D0291985

Ian
and the Great Silver Dragon
Bry-Ankh

IAN

AND
THE

GREAT SILVER DRAGON
BRY-ANKH

◈ **JIM DILYARD** ◈

THE WOOSTER BOOK COMPANY

Wooster Ohio • 2014

The Wooster Book Company
where minds and imaginations meet

Copyright © 2014 Jim Dilyard
  All rights reserved.

No part of this book may be reproduced, utilized, or transmitted in any form or by any means, electronic or mechanical, including photocopying, recording, or by any information storage-and-retrieval system, without permission in writing from the publisher.

The Wooster Book Company
205 West Liberty Street
Wooster, Ohio 44691
www.woosterbook.com

Printed and bound in the United States of America.

Cover and text illustrations by Amy Rottinger.

ISBN: 978-1-59098-648-6

∞ This book is printed on acid-free paper comprising at least 50% post-consumer recycled fiber.

Dedication:

*to the child within,
always seeking someone to love
who will never fail*

Contents

IAN
AND THE GREAT SILVER DRAGON
BRY-ANKH

Introduction

Welcome, dear reader, to an adventure. I am deeply grateful that you have taken time to examine this book. It is my intent to take you on a journey of fantasy and exploration and into the possibilities of "what if." An old Chinese proverb states that a journey of a thousand miles starts with but one step. Is this your first step? Or is it another step on your own personal journey towards knowledge. If so, then congratulations for taking action.

To my young readers, take time to dream as you read because dreams are real things. They have a substance and energy, for they lead the mind into the fun game of exploration and creation. You were created to be a creator from the desires of your own mind and thoughts. You and I are composed of the same elements as the stars in the sky. We are all children of this great and wonderful universe.

There are steps necessary to learn in order to develop what you truly want. To see the desires of your mind come true will become an absolute truth when the recipe for manifesting these desires is correctly followed. There is nothing that you cannot be, do, or have when you have trained your thoughts to work in the correct order. It is truly all about you, the individual. Only you can feel, think, act, and have the emotions that make you unique among all the other people on this exciting and ever-creating world.

Your first and foremost task is always to try to *feel good now,* at this very moment, and to keep trying to feel better. Your fantastically complicated brain is both a transmitter and receiver of energy. What you think and send out *will* return to you. It is a law that cannot be changed or broken. You and I have been using this law our entire lives whether we are aware of its existence and power or not. It is always working because we are always thinking and sending out energy.

We get back what we ask for. The mastery of life is to become aware of what we are asking, and to make the asking process work for happiness and success. It may take five minutes to learn a success principle but it may take a lifetime to master it. We are always on the journey to mastery. It is what we were created to do and it should become the path we choose to follow.

This adventure is a beginning. There will be others. What if the great creator placed other thinking, loving, living creatures here before us? What if they learned the secrets of this world a long time ago? What if they are still here? Perhaps that whisper in your ear is your own personal dragon, one that has been waiting and waiting for you to summon it to your side. Are we the only ones on this amazing home we call Earth who have the ability to create something new and never seen before?

What if—what if—oh, what if?

Acknowledgements

First I want to thank my family. I have shamelessly used them for inspiration and creativity in this small book. Without their support, this story may never have been told. To Janine, who came back for me, I offer a special thanks. A thank you goes out to Pascal for telling me that the story was worth publishing. Diane, Elizabeth, and Beverly for the time they took as proofreaders of earlier manuscripts, I am eternally indebted. Thank you Donna, you told me to find my own voice and encouraged me to keep trying. Amy, your beautiful art has enhanced the story and helped make it real. KT, for helping to bring all of the people and circumstances needed for success into my reality.

To all of you, much love and appreciation.

Chapter One
The Life at Home

WINTER, AND IAN, A YOUNG LAD, is out of school for Christmas break. He is taking a long walk in the woods; the icy cold wind moves the leaf-barren trees in a slow dance back and forth. As they sway, Ian can hear them creak and groan from the cold.

The dry air makes Ian's nose tingle. He exhales the moist air from his lungs and sees the cloud of vapor from his breath. He hears the crunching sound of his boots on the frozen snow while he makes his way through the woods. Mittens keep his hands warm and the scarf around his neck prevents the wind from getting under the heavy winter coat.

Over his ears, he wears a woolen stocking cap his mother made for him so that only his eyes and nose are exposed to the cold wind.

Ian enjoys this time of year. When the wind does not blow, the silence of winter is everywhere. He can think and dream as he walks around the family estate. Dreams of distant places he has read about in books play out in his mind. He can imagine strange-looking animals and birds, hear the roar of lions on the plains of Africa, and the trumpeting of the huge bull elephants. In his imagination, the air vibrates as a thousand water birds take flight at the same time.

Sometimes he dreams of worlds far out in space that are waiting to be discovered, worlds with two suns, or perhaps several moons. Mighty spaceships travel the cold empty distances between planets and stars. The ships connect the inhabitants of one world with another or have terrible weapons and fierce warriors on board.

He envisions intelligent insects or places where the animals and creatures talk to each other. In these places, plants move with the sun and stay green the entire year. He imagines things that might be. In winter especially, he feels magic when he takes the time to look for it.

As he walks, he sees in the distance the neighborhood where he lives and the smoke from coal and wood coming out the many chimneys. Lights in windows remind him of warm rooms and fireplaces. Hot cocoa, with one or two large marshmallows in it, might be waiting for him when he returns from his walk. The thought of cocoa turns his steps back toward home where he can get warmed up. He makes his way out of the woods and starts over the rolling hills toward home. He is aware of the light gray winter sky and the weak sun that casts a small shadow of him as he walks. He smiles at the animal tracks in the snow that mark the presence of nature's winter inhabitants. Even in winter, when the estate seems to be asleep, life is waiting to explode with the coming of spring.

Once inside the house, Ian removes his heavy winter boots and puts them on a wooden rack to dry. On the wall are wooden pegs where he hangs his coat, hat, and mittens. On the floor are wool-lined sheepskin slippers that will make his toes toasty warm. His mother asks him if he is cold. He responds with a quick, "Yes," because this answer increases the chances that hot cocoa will be waiting as he puts on the slippers and skips up the hallway to the kitchen.

On the counter is a fresh cup of cocoa, with two marshmallows swimming in the deep, dark liquid, along with a spoon for stirring. Steam rising from the cup carries the wonderful aroma of cocoa, making Ian's mouth water with expectation. He carefully stirs the mixture and watches as the marshmallows start to melt in the hot brew. When the mix is just right, he uses the spoon to take a sip. The cocoa is absolutely delicious. The process is repeated until the marshmallows are gone, and he drinks the rest of the cup until the cocoa is safely warming his tummy.

The kitchen is one of Ian's favorite places to be. Electric lights cast a glow on the wooden cabinets. Pots and pans hang from metal racks over the counter in the center of the room. On the walls are rows of dishes and numerous cookbooks. The countertops have large glass bottles filled with flour, sugar, rice, salt, pepper, and oatmeal. In the corner is a shelf with lots of little bottles with different spices in them. His mother uses them to add flavor to the meals.

The oatmeal is special because his mother uses it to make breakfast. She adds raisins or brown sugar to the mix and sometimes blueberries. In addition to the oatmeal, a couple of slices of fresh bacon and some buttered toast are a meal fit for a king.

Ian's mother is busy floating about the kitchen getting the evening meal ready for the rest of the family. She is a tall, slender woman with long dark hair and bright green eyes which shine from the inside out. She is wearing a blue apron with yellow flowers along the edges that seem to move on their own. She hums a tune as she does her work. Ian loves his mother very much, and when she smiles a bright crisp smile at him, he gets a warm feeling inside that is not only from the cocoa, and smiles back.

Ian gets up from his stool by the counter and puts his empty mug in the sink. His mother asks him to find his older brother and his father and tell them that dinner will be ready in about an hour. He looks back and gives a quick, "Yes, Mom," and walks past the great black-and-porcelain stove on his way out of the kitchen. He smells the roast chicken in the oven and sees the pans of green beans and potatoes boiling on top. Off to the side is fresh bread waiting to be baked. It is going to be a wonderful dinner.

Ian makes his way up the long hall. At the end is a library which is also his father's office. He enters the library and sees his father behind the large wooden desk. His father is busy reading a report from one of his many businesses.

As Ian nears the desk, his father notices him and puts down the papers, greeting him with a warm smile. Ian's father is a man of medium build, slightly taller than his mother. He is a strong man for his size and Ian can see the well-developed muscles in his arms which come from his days of working in the oil fields. He is a little older for a father than some of Ian's friends' fathers, but that does not bother Ian.

"Son," his father says, "is there something I can do for you?"

Ian looks into his father's blue-gray eyes and simply replies, "Mom says dinner will be ready in about an hour."

"Very good," is the response, and his father waves his hands encouraging Ian to come closer. He reaches out with a quick, firm motion, grabbing Ian with one arm and giving him a big squeeze and then a quick kiss on the top of the forehead. Ian giggles and turns to leave the room. He takes a quick look at the expansive library with its shelves of books. Both his father and mother are avid readers. He sees the technical books about geology and oil-well drilling, the romance novels Ian's mother loves to read, and the section of books on ancient civilizations, science, and mathematics. Another set of shelves holds fun books: mysteries, science fiction, and all kinds of things in between. It is a wonderful place to be when the weather is too bad to be outside.

Ian heads back down the long hall and starts up the winding stairs to the bedrooms in search of his brother. As he approaches his brother's room, he hears soft rock-and-roll music coming from behind the closed door. He opens the door and enters the forbidden zone that is his brother's room. His brother looks up from his homework and gives him a smirk and asks, "What do you want, twerp?"

Ian gives a quick look around the poorly lit room that smells of dirty socks and unwashed clothes. "Mom says dinner will be ready in about an hour, and you need to wash up before you can come to eat."

"No, I don't. Now get out of here, twerp, and shut the door behind you before I put your head in my trashcan."

Ian does an about-face and, just before he leaves the room, he turns and sticks out his tongue. The door shuts and he hears a loud thud as a book hits the other side. Ian and his brother have a love-hate relationship which is mostly on the "hate" side right now. His mother says teenagers are not much fun and his brother fills the bill completely.

Chapter Two
A Place for Dreams

IAN WALKS TO HIS ROOM at the other end of the upstairs hall which is as far from his brother's room as possible. It is not quite as large but it is much cleaner-smelling and the lights are brighter. Ian has his own books and toys to play with. He likes to build metal cars and trucks from his erector set with his father's help. Plastic soldiers and warriors which look like they come from distant worlds are assembled one piece at a time until they seem almost lifelike. He then places them in mock battles using imagined weapons. Ian finds tremendous fun in building them any way he wants.

An easel with drawing paper stands next to his telescope in one corner of the room. Ian is very good at drawing. He draws anything from dinosaurs to spaceships. He will sometimes draw pictures of what he believes houses of the future will look like. Some are tall with lots of glass and use sunlight for warmth. Others are low and close to the ground and let the earth shield them from the weather and cold. He has heard his father talk about the need to be mindful of keeping a balance between the needs of people and the needs of the environment. His father says it is necessary to be a good steward of natural resources.

Ian has books about dinosaurs and creatures from long ago. He learned the names of many dinosaurs, such as the three-horned Triceratops, the long-necked Apatosaurus, and the blood-dripping teeth of the mighty Tyrannosaurs rex; the fleet-footed Velociraptors that hunted in packs

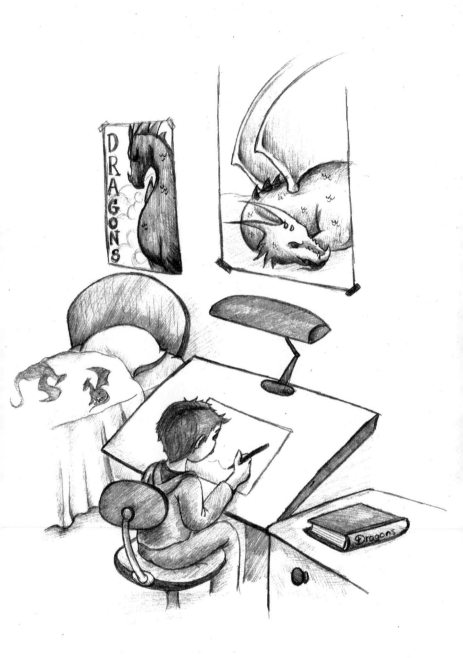

like wolves, and the high-flying Pterodactyls with leathery wings and long rows of small sharp teeth. Evidence of so many others can be seen in the fossil record of the Earth.

Ian has other books about ancient Egypt and Greece, especially Athens, the once-mighty capital of Greece and the birthplace of democracy. Zeus, Apollo, Mercury, and the champion Hercules are all alive in the pages of his books. Egyptian slaves can be seen building the Great Pyramid and the mysterious Sphinx. Ian pretends to be pharaoh and rule the entire ancient world, his kingdom stretching from the banks of the Nile to the mountains of Nubia. He likes to read about the myths and legends of the Old World.

Ian has one particular set of books that are different from the others. His mother gave these books to him for a special reason. She noticed, at times, that he would go into periods of unusual quiet and sadness because there was no one his own age to play with living close to home. This is one of the reasons he likes to read so much and also because his brother is just too old to be a playmate.

During one of Ian's sad times, his mother, who was in town shopping, stopped at the local bookstore in search of an interesting book for Ian to read. There, on a somewhat dusty shelf, she saw a large set of books about dragons. She thought to herself that Ian might enjoy reading about dragons because they are totally imagined creatures, and Ian does have a wonderful imagination. She brought them home and his life changed.

Ian became unexpectedly obsessed with dragons. Suddenly dragons were everywhere. He could see them in his mind, out in the woods, or flying just out of sight behind a low hill. The clouds in the sky were only there to hide the dragons which soared in the high, cold air. Dragons are on his bed sheets and comforters. Pictures of all the different kinds of dragons are pinned to the walls of his bedroom. Ian draws them on his art paper and attaches the pictures to the easel. On one shelf in his room is a model of a fierce-looking dragon he made out of plastic pieces. The same pieces that he used to make his space warriors.

Ian is just getting ready to set up his telescope to look out the window for a dragon when he hears his mother calling for both he and his brother to come down for dinner. He had almost forgotten about the small feast waiting for everyone in the kitchen. When he is in his room, Ian mostly thinks about dragons.

Chapter Three
Believing

IAN WAITS TO MAKE SURE his brother is first down the stairs before leaving his room. He takes a quick look around the room, then tells his dragons he will be back soon. The door closes and he heads for the kitchen.

The smell of the freshly-prepared meal is delightful and he now realizes that his appetite is very big and very real. The family gathers around the square kitchen table in their regular chairs. The table is set with colorful plates and dishes. An embroidered white tablecloth covers the table and cloth napkins hold the silverware. Ian sees fresh milk in his glass. The chicken that was roasting in the oven is a golden brown and Ian's father is busy slicing off pieces and handing them around. Fresh, warm vegetables, potatoes, and bread are placed strategically on the table. A pitcher of cold water sits ready. Fresh flowers fill a vase in the center of the table.

Before they start to eat, Ian's father bows his head and says a short prayer of thanks. He often tells them that they should be grateful and thankful for the food and possessions they have. The great Creator is blessing them in many ways.

The meal is wonderful and Ian eats more than enough to satisfy his appetite. The discussion around the table usually has to do with current events or an incident from the newspaper. A local farmer reported that some of his cattle have gone missing and cannot be found. Ian's brother is saying that UFOs are to blame, while his mother believes more convincingly in broken fences. Father has a comment about the potential for thieves

in the middle of the night. Ian however is thinking that dragons might be looking for a tasty meal. He looks up from the finished meal and says to his father, "What if it was a dragon?"

His father gives back a slight smile and Mother just shakes her head and has that "oh my" expression.

Ian's brother is quick to give Ian a death glare and a negative response. "Ian, you and your stupid dragons! Don't you know by now that they aren't even real?"

Before another word is spoken, Ian's father looks directly at his older son and says, "If Ian wants to think that a dragon may be the reason for the problem, then that is okay. If you will remember, there was a time when you believed in the Easter Bunny and the Tooth Fairy."

The brother's face becomes bright red with anger but the look he gets from his father is telling him not to say another word. His father continues, "Besides, you don't know what you don't know. Until there is actual proof one way or another, a dragon could exist. After all, the world is a very big place."

Ian is relieved that his father has come to his defense. The argument about dragons not being real and that they are just legends or myths does not dampen his belief in the possibility of at least one real dragon somewhere in the world.

With a short lull in the conversation, Ian's mother asks everyone to help clear the table and put the dishes in the sink and dishwasher. Ian is happy to lend a hand but he keeps an eye out for his embarrassed brother. He knows that at the right moment retaliation will be coming his way. You cannot get away with winning one over on your older brother without paying a price.

The last dish is finished and Ian delights his mother with a big hug. She responds with her own hug and kisses him on top of the head. With this, Ian turns and tells everyone he is going up to his room. Ian makes a quick scan of the room and with the coast clear heads up the stairs and back into the realm of dragons. He shuts the door quickly and, just for precaution, locks it. He does not want to be ambushed by you-know-who.

Ian turns on the reading light next to his bed and grabs a large picture book of dragons turning pages full of different dragons. Dragons of Gold, Copper, Bronze, Brass, and Silver jump from the pages and into his imagination: Earth dragons of Fire, Wind, Water, Wood, and Stone Dragons that live in the lands of China and Japan; India Sky Dragons that roam the high mountains of the Himalayas; and Ice Dragons from the North and South Poles that are rare and hardly ever seen. An entire culture of dragons lives in these books. He loves to read about them and believes that his deepest, secret desire to someday meet a real dragon will come true.

Mother calls up the steps for both boys to get ready for bed, interrupting Ian on his imaginary dragon journey. She reminds them, as she does every night, to brush their teeth and wash their faces before putting on their pajamas. Ian heads for the bathroom down the hall between the bedrooms. The light in the bathroom is off which means it is safe to enter. Ian is sure his brother is cooking up some diabolical plan and wants to avoid being turned upside down with his head in a trashcan. With his mission accomplished, Ian is back in his room in a flash.

He is not quite sleepy yet so he goes to the window and scans the countryside with his telescope. In the cold and crisp night air a half-moon hangs low in the western sky. The looking glass points toward a series of rolling hills just outside of the woods. It is a perfect place for a dragon to be sitting and looking for an unsuspecting meal. However, on this night Ian does not see any movement or any shapes that could be a dragon, so he puts the telescope back and slips under the thick blanket, decorated with dragons, where he is comfortably warm and asleep in a few short minutes.

Chapter Four
Dreams and Dragons

IAN DREAMS THIS NIGHT about dragons and sees all different kinds and knows something about each one's distinctive look and personality. A Gold Dragon that stands twenty feet tall, almost to the top a two-story house, comes to greet him. The large, delicately gold-coated wings, when fully extended, cover a football field from side to side. Large, dark eyes indicate the dragon's deep knowledge and ability to understand. A Gold Dragon is dedicated to fighting injustice and to protecting the people it cares for from evil. The head of a Gold Dragon is sleek and well-rounded. Looking at a Gold Dragon, a person is soon put at ease. These dragons have such a kind and assuring appearance and they are so polite in conversation that they instantly become your friend.

Two types of dragons exist. The first group are the good dragons that will help people and teach them. The other group of dragons are the tricksters and deceivers. They do not help people and are only interested in getting treasure for themselves. The color or type of dragon does not indicate which one it is. The only way to tell good from bad is to listen closely to them as they speak. A bad dragon speaks with a voice that sounds like the hiss of a snake because it has a forked tongue. A good dragon has perfect speech and a straight tongue.

Ian says goodnight to the Gold Dragon and it bows its head to him in a sign of respect and takes its leaves. A Brass Dragon gently glides down from the sky. It bows its head, acknowledging Ian and giving him a

gentle smile. This dragon is smaller than the Gold Dragon at sixteen feet tall. The shiny brass-covered wings at full extension reach almost sixty feet. The bright brass color of the dragon reminds Ian of his trumpet. Brass Dragons do not say much and this one is no exception. It opens its wings and with a few powerful moves is once more heading skyward. Ian waves his hand and the dragon rolls over in flight as if to say, "Thank you."

Ian watches as the Brass Dragon gets smaller in the distance then Ian feels a small vibration from the ground behind him. He turns to see a beautiful Bronze Dragon folding in its wings. Bronze Dragons are masterful shape-shifters. They can change into all kinds of creatures. Perhaps it is necessary to be a furry little rabbit or a large black bear. A Bronze Dragon can be an eagle or a swiftly swimming whale. Bronze Dragons are quite happy taking on different shapes. It allows them to help humans without the person being afraid of the dragon. This particular dragon lowers its head and Ian rubs its delicate horns. The dragon purrs like a kitten and Ian smiles at the idea of a dragon being a cat. Suddenly, after a burst of blue light, the dragon is a large, yellow tabby cat. It rubs around Ian's leg and quickly bounces out of sight in search of an unsuspecting mouse.

Looking up for more dragon friends, Ian sees a Copper Dragon low in the sky. It is not heading in his direction which is okay. Copper Dragons are usually bad dragons and are known to trick people. They have a clever wit and are very proud of their ability to make crafty jokes and tricks. If a Copper Dragon speaks to you, be sure to listen for the slight hiss in its voice and be aware. If it can trick you, it will. A Copper Dragon is fond of treasures and will go to great lengths to cheat you out of yours. Ian knows to be polite with any dragon but to be ready for any suspicious activity.

Ian is quite pleased with his visitors tonight but he has not yet seen his very favorite dragon of all. Ian sits on a large, flat-topped rock and looks skyward and searches. There is nothing in the distance or in the high sky. He is about to give up looking when a strange smell drifts his way. The odor reminds him of a fresh spring rain. He turns toward the source of the smell and is briefly blinded by a short, bright flash of pure white light. Ian blinks several times to refocus his eyes. As his vision clears, Ian sees before him a magnificent sight. Sitting comfortably on the ground a few feet away is the most perfect Silver Dragon he has ever seen. Ian is ecstatic. A Silver Dragon is the dragon that Ian most wants to get to know.

Hopping down from his rock, Ian bows respectfully to the huge dragon in front of him. The dragon does not move except to curl its long tail around its massive four feet.

Ian is so happy to finally see a Silver Dragon that he is temporarily speechless.

Ian carefully looks and studies the dragon. He has read that a Silver Dragon can be twenty-two feet tall and stretch its wings to over one hundred and fifty feet. Silver Dragons are the true fliers of the dragon world. They can glide in the cold, high air for days at a time and never get tired.

A Silver Dragon is the most respected of all the dragons. They are shape-shifters like the Bronze Dragons but will keep a shape for years. A Silver Dragon is a tireless worker for the humans in its care. They are always on the side of justice and goodness. To be befriended by a Silver Dragon is a great honor.

Ian has regained his voice and is about to say something to his new friend when the dragon suddenly speaks first and says simply, "Good evening, my dear Ian."

Ian cannot get a word out as his mouth is frozen half open, half shut. The dragon continues to look at him with its bright red eyes curling its lips into a wonderful, assuring smile. Ian's mind is racing, "It knows my name! How can that be?" With this thought, there is another flash of bright white light and the Silver Dragon is gone.

Ian awakens in his bed with a rush of energy and quickly looks around the room. He realizes that he just had a wonderful dream. He tries to go back to sleep but he cannot. His only thought is, "It knows my name. I saw a Silver Dragon and it knows who I am." What a wild and special dream! Eventually Ian falls back to sleep, but the vividness of the dream remains.

Chapter Five
The Dragon Knew His Name

A SUNNY AND COLD DAY greets Ian as he awakens from his night of dragon dreams. He still remembers all of the dragons he met, especially the great silver one which he saw last. The sound of his name spoken by the Silver Dragon is still fresh in his mind. He knows it is a dream but the possibility of a dragon friend is just too good to pass up.

Ian heads downstairs to the kitchen. Today, his mother is making pancakes with blueberries in them. The maple syrup on the table comes from the sugar maple trees on the estate. Ian is the first one downstairs. He gets two fresh pancakes and adds just a little syrup. He eats his breakfast quickly because he is still expecting his brother to get even with him. His brother is not an early riser and is usually in a sour mood in the morning. Today, Ian is lucky so he decides to tell his mother about his dream. "Mom, you'll never guess what I dreamed about last night."

"Well, if I am never going to guess then it would be best if you told me what all the excitement is about," his mother responds.

"I had a great dream about meeting dragons. And one of them knew my name!"

"Well," says his mother, "that is indeed an interesting dream. Did this dragon have anything else to tell you?"

Ian quickly replies, "No, not really. Before I could ask him a question, he just vanished in a pop of bright light and was gone. He is the most beautiful dragon that I've ever seen and the best part is that he is a Silver Dragon which is my favorite dragon of all."

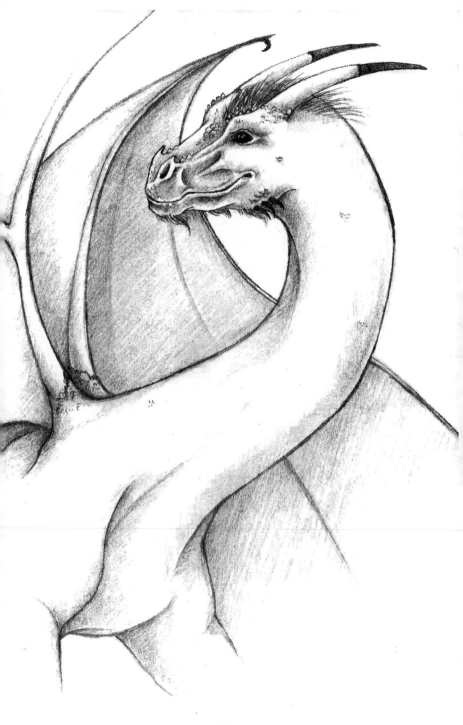

With this statement Ian's mother smiles at him and reminds him that dreams are dreams and what is in them is usually not real. Ian understands her politeness about dragons not being real. He places his breakfast dishes on the counter by the sink and, since he is still in his pajamas, bounces back up the stairs to the dragon sanctuary of his bedroom. He thinks about the dream and how the dragon knew his name.

Ian finds his book about Silver Dragons and once more looks at the pictures and reads the stories. A Silver Dragon, like most dragons, lives in clans. A clan is a group of dragons that are related to each other and are of the same kind; however, adult dragons sometimes choose to live a solitary life. A Silver Dragon is wise and a great teacher. As a champion of justice, it will protect the person it has chosen to teach and work with.

To look at a Silver Dragon is to see a living, moving piece of perfection. The silver scales of the dragon are so close together that they look like molten silver as it moves. In flight, the Silver Dragon is smooth and long. It moves as fast as a meteor flashing through the night sky and can be just as bright. Two horns on the dragon's head lean backwards at a fifteen-degree angle which is the perfect angle for high-altitude flying. Each horn is about two feet long with the last six inches jet black in color. Black on the horns of a dragon is an indicator of the dragon's honesty and great integrity.

The magnificent horns of the Silver Dragon are not its only mark of distinction. On the top of the dragon's head is a frill or comb of soft silver hair that is also tipped in black. Like the horns, the frill is also at a fifteen-degree angle but will flatten when the dragon is in flight. On the underside of the Silver Dragon's mouth is another frill but this one is made up of fine, red hair. This color of red is the same as its flashing eyes. A Silver Dragon is considered a good dragon and has a straight, smooth tongue. It is the most truthful of all dragons. When its mouth is closed, no teeth show which allows a Silver Dragon to smile at you just by curling its lips. This smile is most calming when such a magnificent dragon decides to show itself to a human.

Ian remembers the dream and the wonderful smile. He wishes that he could meet this dragon again. He continues to read about the dragon's home.

A dragon's home is called a lair. Lairs are usually in high, secluded places where the dragon can rest and do its studies. A lair has several cavernous rooms in it such as a library, a clinic, a laboratory, a sleeping chamber, and of course a treasure room. Some lairs have a guest room for visitors to stay in. A dragon that has chosen to work with a person will sometimes take him to its home. To be allowed into a dragon's lair is a high honor.

The library in the lair is where the complete history of the dragon clan is kept. All of the names of the known dragons of the clan are listed. A dragon is proud of its clan's linage. Books and ancient scrolls fill the shelves with dragon philosophy, mathematics, science, art, and history. Some of the clan's history is written in jewels that date back to the time of the dinosaurs. Dragons are ancient creatures and have lived in peace for millions of years.

The clinic and laboratory are usually combined into one room. The lab has bubbling bottles of potions along with flowers and herbs which it uses to make medicines. Mirrors are positioned on the ceiling and walls to bring in fresh sunlight to keep the plants healthy. Bookshelves have volumes of medical information for both dragons and humans; these books are available for doing research and to find just the right medicine in a time of need. A dragon is a great student of the healing arts.

A Silver Dragon's bedroom is really just a sleeping chamber. A dragon does not sleep on a bed like a person. The room has a floor covered with very fine and colorful carpets. A sleeping dragon will rest comfortably on its feet with its tail wrapped around its body. It will then lay its long neck and head in the opposite direction of the tail. A sleeping dragon has the look of a large coil of rope that is alive. The chamber does not have much furniture but has a place for aromatic oils and candles. Dragons love fragrances and the smell of wildflowers. Light in the chamber comes from small torches on the wall. Although the main purpose of the chamber is for resting, there is little need for brightness even during daylight hours.

The last room of the lair is the most important room of all. It is the treasure room. Every dragon has a treasure room in which it keeps the items it collects over its lifetime. A Silver Dragon likes beautifully crafted jewelry and finely woven fabric. Fine gem stones and wonderful art and sculpture are located in open places for viewing. Treasure brings a dragon much enjoyment when in its lair. A Silver Dragon will have a few pieces of gold and silver, but they are usually in the form of artwork or rare coins. Some of the items can be used for teaching tools such as when helping their human students understand the great truths and laws of this world and the universe. A treasure room will always be brightly lit with torches that never go out. A dragon likes to look at its treasure but it does not covet it. A dragon's treasure reminds it of special events from earlier in its life. Treasure tells the history of the dragon which is why it is so special to the dragon and its clan.

A Silver Dragon is indeed a great and magnificent dragon and is looked upon with both admiration and splendor. A Silver Dragon is what Ian dreamed of and someday hopes to meet. The dream of the night before is still fresh in his mind, and Ian remembers that the dragon knew his name.

Ian sits back on his bed and thinks about how his family keeps telling him that dragons are not real, and that they are only his imagination. The books he has read are not real stories but only myths and legends. This makes Ian sad at times. He wants so much to believe in dragons and in the wisdom they possess. He does not know why he has such a strong belief in dragons, but he does. He knows that somewhere in the world there is at least one dragon and that someday he will meet that dragon.

His mother calls up the stairs for him to get dressed and to come down to the kitchen. She has some errands to do and needs the help of a strong young man. He puts away his dragon books and dresses quickly. Having errands to do usually means that something fun may happen but it will be a mystery until he sets out with his mother.

Ian and his mother put on their winter coats and head out for an adventure in the pickup truck. Riding in the truck means the errands might include getting bulk food or building materials or new young animals for the estate. What if they stop at the library and find more dragon books to read? Ian is going to have a wonderful day and is happy to be with his mother. They sing songs as they ride into town and Ian thinks less about dragons and more about the fun of today's activities which are still a mystery. However new and exciting the day is though, Ian can still hear in his mind the words of the dragon who knew his name, "Good evening, my dear Ian." It is a reminder of dreams yet to be fulfilled.

Chapter Six
The Beginning

SUMMER ON THE ESTATE. Gone are the cold and snow of winter and the rain and ever-present mud of spring. Life has fully returned with the leaves on the trees and with crops in the fields. Winter wheat is nearly ready to harvest. Corn and soybeans have been recently planted in the fields. The first cutting of hay will be ready soon. Cattle enjoy the fresh summer grass and the horses frisk about in the pasture.

Studies and classes from school are over for a while and it is a time for fun, relaxation, and adventure. Walks around the estate now include views of mother deer with their new fawns. Squirrels and chipmunks scamper around the oak trees. Fish swim in the lake and jump into the air to catch low-flying insects. Adventures and opportunities for increased knowledge are available all around the estate.

Ian and his brother have summer chores to do. Ian's chores mostly involve looking after the animals. His brother helps the other farm hands run equipment and mend items that have weathered poorly through the past winter. Ian finds that he has more free time than his brother each day and spends that time reading books or drawing.

The courtyard behind the house provides a great place to read. Ian's mother has filled it with flowers, hedges, and ornamental bushes. The courtyard has geometric designs that are made of different kinds of stepping stones. In the center is a large spiral walkway that ends at a beautiful multi-level water fountain. Flowers and bushes along the walkway hide

the fountain from view until the very end. The sight is breathtaking, especially at night when colored lights illuminate the cascading water.

Stone benches are strategically placed in and around the courtyard as are several large rocks. One of these rocks, unearthed from the estate, is so large that Ian's father had a stone mason carve out a place in it in which a person can sit. It is a great place to read a book or to daydream. The rock stores heat from the summer sun which makes it a warm and relaxing spot to sit.

On the right side of the courtyard is the heated swimming pool. The pool area is where Ian's brother's friends stay when they come for a visit. They play video games, tell stories, listen to music, bash each other about in the water, and eat volumes of food. Ian's mother is constantly telling them that they are eating all of her food allowance. The words seem to fall on deaf ears because the food always shows up and is consumed. They are grateful but of course never admit it.

Ian does not associate with them because they tell him they are older and more sophisticated and do not need his presence. He is not an older teenager and could not possibly relate to their lives. The truth is, he is just fine with this situation. He would much rather read and dream on his own. Dragons that live in his mind and on paper keep expanding his imagination. He is happy in his own world.

Ian's morning chores are finished. The animals are in good shape with plenty of water and fresh grain or grass to eat. The day is sunny with warm temperatures and a slight puff of wind every now and then. He goes into the kitchen to find his mother making a lunch of grilled cheese sandwiches to go along with homemade chicken soup. He eats his cheese sandwich with a glass of cold milk.

There are no chores for the afternoon so he gives his mother a quick hug and goes up to his room. It is a good day for reading. He finds his favorite book on Silver Dragons and takes the book to the courtyard and finds the big rock that is shaped for sitting. The rock is already warm from the morning sun. The warmth soaks into him as he begins to read once more about magnificent Silver Dragons. The gentleness of the afternoon relaxes him and makes him drowsy, and before long, Ian falls asleep with the dragon book still in his hands.

Ian dreams about his many dragon friends. Gold, Brass, and Earth Dragons come by to say hello and give him a smile or a friendly nod. He thinks he sees a Silver Dragon high in the sky but it is too far away for him to be sure. He is happy to be sharing some time with his dragons.

All of a sudden Ian sees then feels a blinding

white light. The intensity of the flash startles him awake from his nap. He rubs his eyes, realizing he has fallen asleep. His dragon book is beside him on the rock, but he feels peculiar. A special odor is in the air. It smells like fresh spring rain but it is not raining nor is it springtime. The odor is somehow familiar to him but he cannot remember when he last smelled it. As he focuses his thoughts, Ian notices that he is covered by a large shadow.

How odd, he thinks. Had he been napping so long that the weather changed? When he went out to read, the day was sunny without a cloud in the sky. Perhaps something changed; after all the smell of rain is still in the air. Ian hops off of his warm rock chair and looks in the direction of the sun, looking for clouds in the sky. His vision is not greeted by clouds but something far greater. A huge creature is blocking the sun! Ian suddenly recognizes the shape of a dragon!

What he sees is not possible. There is no such thing as a dragon! Ian has been told over and over that dragons are not real. He must be dreaming. Dragons are only myths or a part of a person's imagination. But here one is, right in front of him. He freezes with fear and excitement at the same time. Ian does not know what to do.

At that moment, the dragon folds its great wings together, looks at Ian, and sits down quietly on its tail. The sun behind the dragon makes it shine like a finely polished mirror. Could it be that this dragon sitting in front of him is a Silver Dragon? As soon as he thinks this thought, the dragon lowers its great head and smiles at him with one of the most pleasant and loving smiles Ian has ever seen. It is almost as nice as his mother's smile. Ian is astonished. The dragon is smiling at him and seems to be able to understand what he is thinking.

Chapter Seven
A Formal Introduction

IAN HEARS WORDS SOUNDING in his mind and they say, "Good afternoon, my dear Ian." He is still frozen motionless but the words seem familiar. He then remembers that he has heard them before. It was his wonderful winter dream where a Silver Dragon knew his name. Could that dream have been telling him of a future event? Is it possible that the dragon in front of him is that very same dragon?

Ian looks at the dragon and once again he hears words in his head. "Do not be afraid, my dear friend Ian. I am the dragon of your dream. I will not harm you. My name is Bry-Ankh, and I am a Silver Dragon of the Clan of Ankh. You believe in dragons with so much passion that it is safe for me to reveal to you that dragons are real and a part of this world."

Ian is still thinking about the wonderful smile and the fact that the dragon knows his name. It takes him a moment to realize that the dragon is also speaking to him. "Did you speak to me? Are you really real and did you speak to me?"

Bry-Ankh looks Ian in the eyes and replies, "It is me, dear Ian, the dragon that you see. I have the ability to speak to you in your own language. I have many abilities and speech is just one of them. You wanted a special friend and I am that friend. I am also a teacher and mentor, if you will allow me to be."

Ian relaxes a little bit. He feels his breathing settling back to normal as well as the rapid beating of his heart slowing. "But how can you be real? Dragons are not supposed to exist. I am just day-dreaming

about them for the fun of it, and here you are. What am I to do now? What if someone sees you or hears me talking to a creature that looks like, like a dragon? People will think I am out of my mind or that I am seeing imaginary creatures."

Bry-Ankh just looks at Ian through his bright red eyes and smiles that wonderful smile, and all of Ian's questions no longer seem important. Bry-Ankh replies, "Dear Ian, do not be worried, for when I am with you, no one else will be able to see or hear us. As far as other people are concerned, the time I spend with you will not be noticed. Dragons know how to control time and can only be seen and heard by the people we want to communicate with. No one but the two of us will know of our friendship. That is, of course, if you are willing to spend time with a dragon?"

Ian, still slightly stunned from this sudden turn of events, does not know what to think.

He has no answer for this question because the idea of a real dragon is just too much to understand. Here he is, seeing this huge creature, and it is talking to him and telling him to relax and accept what is being offered.

Ian takes a long, deep breath and says, "Bry-Ankh, how do I know that you are real and not my imagination? Can you prove to me that you are what and who you say you are?"

Bry-Ankh continues to smile and makes himself a little more comfortable. His long tail curls up around his legs. "Ian, I can show you a world of things and places from the past and even some of the possible future. All that it will take from you is a little trust."

Ian looks Bry-Ankh in the eyes and once again sees that loving smile. He finds it impossible to say no.

Bry-Ankh leans closer to Ian and tells him, "Close your eyes and keep them closed. I will tap you on the head with one of my claws."

Ian sits with his eyes closed and feels a gentle touch on his head and then his mind seems to explode with color and sound.

Chapter Eight
Worlds Past and Future

IAN FINDS HIMSELF FLOATING high above a blue planet where water surrounds a single, large mass of dry land. On this land are all kinds of animals that Ian knows are dinosaurs. He sees herds of Apatosaurs. Triceratops and Stegosaurs are in the lush foliage looking for fresh water. Raptors lurk in the shadows and a Tyrannosaurs rex swiftly chases down a fleeing Iguanodon. Ian thinks he sees Pterodactyls flying in the air and some fliers which resemble dragons. Dragons. Now this is an interesting sight to possibly be seeing dragons along with dinosaurs. Ian also sees that the oceans are filled with so many marine creatures that he cannot count them all.

The world is warm, animals and plants are everywhere. All at once the land and the sea explode in such violence that mountains turn into volcanoes shooting flame and dust into the air. The land mass splits into seven pieces that move across the waters and the seas fill in the spaces between the lands. Some of the dinosaurs do not survive but others take their place. The climate changes many times and the air changes from clear to dirty from the dust of volcanoes then back to clear. The plants and animals live and die and live again.

Ian realizes that he is watching the cycle of life and death upon the Earth. He sees the animals change over time as they grow large during times when there is abundant plant life and then become small when plants are few and the land is dry.

Ian looks out at the stars that shower the Earth with the soft light of night and notices a large object coming toward the Earth. The object is a large space rock that strikes with such force that it turns day into night and shakes the planet. Huge waves form in the seas and wash over the land with destruction. Many of the dinosaurs die right away. The rest of them die later as do most of the plants. The dust in the air from the impact of the huge rock blocks the sun and turns the Earth cold and dark.

Ian is saddened by all the destruction but as before, he notices that life in the sea and plants on the land start to grow again. As the plants grow, the animal life returns, but this time the animals are different. Gone are the old dinosaurs of the past. New animal life flourishes on the earth. In the air, creatures fly that are somewhat like the old flying dinosaurs. He looks closely at these fliers and they look familiar. Some of them have feathers similar to the birds of his time but he sees another presence in the sky. Yes, it is true. They are dragons! They survived the extinction which happened to the dinosaurs. All sizes, shapes, and colors fill the air. They fly with such grace and agility that is simply amazing to watch.

The Earth continues changing as the seven land masses move farther apart and the top and bottom of the Earth become covered in ice and snow. All through the natural cycle of the Earth, the only constant are the living dragons. They are watching and learning and understanding the nature of the Earth and the stars above the Earth. They are becoming wise.

Ian sees another form of life start to flourish on the lands of the Earth, the first humans. They are small at first and live in caves and are hunters of the abundant wildlife. The early humans learn to make tools and weapons. They become competent at killing game for food and, regretfully, they also learn to fight each other. With time they start to form small villages and learn to grow crops in the fields. These villages grow and become small towns and then bigger cities. The primitive impulse that humans have for fighting does not leave them. They start to have fights with each other and neighboring villages and cities. The fights turn into wars and Ian sees large and small armies of men attack each other across different parts of the world. Always, above all the violence, the dragons are watching.

The world does what it will always do. The cycles of nature are not affected by the efforts of men. Ian sees men build large cities in the deserts and along rivers and then destroy them in wars which seem to increase in violence and destruction. He is aware that while the great cities are being built, the dragons fly around the cities, but when the wars start, the dragons leave the sky. Ian puzzles about this curious event and why the dragons come and go.

He feels a great sadness in his heart as he watches men build cities and then states and countries all over the planet just to destroy them at a later date. He does not understand why humans have this great desire to destroy the wonderful things they build. As Ian watches the view of the world turn and change beneath him, he sees what appears to be his own time and how things look in the present. Just as fast as he views his own time, the Earth moves forward and the scenes change again. This time the cities and countries are huge and the human population of the Earth appears like a colony of ants. So many people with transportation devices move around the ground and sea and air. There is motion everywhere and people are moving faster and faster. The cities glow at night with their light brighter than the stars and no one seems to take time to rest or stop.

As before, wars still start. But now the wars are worldwide with death and destruction on a massive scale. Men fight each other with powerful armies and the nations are leveled to the ground only to be rebuilt once again.

Ian watches this cycle and hopes with all his heart that it will end and humans will learn to live in peace as the dragons do. He wants people to value life and to enjoy the things of beauty that they make. Something is preventing this from happening and Ian wants to know what this something is. As he is thinking these thoughts, Ian sees objects fly into the air from all the countries of the Earth. He watches these small darts which look like flying torches arch across the sky and then start to fall back to the Earth on different nations or cities. When the darts land, they explode with a blinding flash of light. Each city is instantly destroyed. The sky grows dark with death and destruction as huge mushroom-shaped clouds rise into the dirty air. The clouds spread all over the earth and everything underneath them dies.

Ian's eyes tear up and his heart feels so heavy with this last and final picture. This time, nothing returns to the Earth, not even the dragons. The planet is still and lifeless. The Sun does what it has always done, and the rain and the snow return to the Earth, but not life. Humans destroy everything that was alive. What a tragedy to occur in such a beautiful place.

Chapter Nine
Hope and Play

DEVASTATED BY WHAT HE HAS JUST SEEN, Ian does not know what to think. Then he feels the slightest tap on his head. His eyes snap open and he is once again at his home in his garden with a dragon.

Ian feels frustrated, mad, sad, and full of questions, all at the same time. Bry-Ankh looks at him and smiles. He seems to smile a lot, Ian thinks.

Then Bry-Ankh says to him, "Ian, you have just seen and felt the history of this planet you call Earth. Most of what you experienced is the past and is very real and accurate. However, the last things you saw were what could come about in a possible future. These events can be changed and humankind does not have to destroy itself and everything else. You see we dragons are sworn to help humans if they ask us. You have asked to see a dragon and am I not here with you now? We dragons, as you see, have been on this planet for a very long time. We learned a long time ago how to act with each other and with the rest of the life forms on Earth in a peaceful way. We learned to develop our minds and to understand the forces of nature and the stars in the sky.

"We became what are called *conscience beings*. I know these are big words and maybe you do not understand what they mean. I will explain some of them each time we meet. It will take a lot of meetings but the rest of the world around you will notice nothing. Remember, we dragons can control time."

Ian takes a deep breath and a great sigh of relief leaves his body. He does not understand

everything Bry-Ankh is saying but he feels in his heart that the words are true and honest.

Bry-Ankh continues, "The dragons of the Earth learned to live in peace by applying a technique called *integrated thinking*. From this way of thinking, we discovered how to get to the essence of things. You see, dragons have a two-sided brain. It is the same kind of brain that humans have, with two parts, or chambers. It is made up of a left and right side, and each side has the ability to communicate with the other. I know this is difficult to understand right now but you need to know how your brain works and how it looks at the rest of the world around you.

"I will explain these ideas to you in more detail later. For now, I want to leave you with one last thought. Dragons made up a code of conduct that we use when we interact with other dragons. We use the same code for interacting with humans. A code is a set of rules which we agree to live by. The code is this:

Rule 1: No dragon or group of dragons may initiate force, threat of force, or fraud against a dragon or the property of a dragon

Rule 2: Force may be used only in defense against any dragon who violates Rule 1

Rule 3: No exceptions shall ever exist to Rules 1 and 2

"These are the rules that we dragons live by and we use the same rules when teaching or working with humans. It is our hope that someday humans will use the same code in their lives."

Ian's head is swimming with all the ideas that Bry-Ankh has just told him and he is confused. He asks, "Bry-Ankh, how will I ever learn and understand all these things? There are so many ideas and the words do not make sense to me. All that I have seen and heard makes me believe that people are bad and they make things that in the end they will only destroy."

Bry-Ankh looks at Ian with so much love in his eyes that Ian cannot help but see how much Bry-Ankh cares. "Ian, all people have the ability to love just as I love you and your family loves you. They just need to learn how to find that love inside themselves and then share it with others. The best way to find that love is through the creation of values which they can give to others. The act of creating opens the door of love that is inside everyone. But that is enough for now. You have seen and learned a lot of new and exciting things today, so now it is time to play."

Ian is so glad to hear the word play. He really wants to have some fun. "What shall we do?" asks Ian.

"How about a game of tag?" replies Bry-Ankh. "But remember, we dragons can change shape!"

And with that last word there is a small bright flash of white light and Bry-Ankh turns into the most beautiful butterfly that Ian has ever seen. "Catch me if you can!" and off the butterfly flies across the garden with Ian laughing and running after him.

Ian's mother hears the laughing coming from the courtyard and looks out the window and sees her young son running after a very pretty butterfly. She thinks, "My, what a lovely sight," and smiles the smile which only mothers can make and watches Ian play.

JIM DILYARD is a life long resident of Wayne County, Ohio. He is married with two sons, two dogs, and two cats. Jim is the owner and president of J D Producing, Inc., and a long time member of the Ohio Oil and Gas Association. He has spent the last thirty-five years producing crude oil and natural gas from the north central area of Ohio. Jim is a senior member of the Professional Bowlers Association and the 2010–2011 winner of the Pat Paterson Award for the Central Region of the PBA. He is also a member of several societies with an interest in developing concepts for personal growth and achievement.